Bluestone

Safe Harbor

Fathomless Sea

Providence
Prominence

Sand Plains of White

The Great Deep

N
W   E
S

A GIFT FOR

FROM

MAX LUCADO

Coming Home

ILLUSTRATIONS BY JUSTIN GERARD

CROSSWAY BOOKS · WHEATON, ILLINOIS

A PUBLISHING MINISTRY OF GOOD NEWS PUBLISHERS

PUBLISHER'S ACKNOWLEDGMENT

The publisher wishes to acknowledge that the text for *Coming Home* appeared originally as "Before It's Too Late" in *Tell Me the Story*, written by Max Lucado and illustrated by Ron DiCianni. Special thanks to Ron DiCianni for the idea and vision behind the creation of the "Tell Me" series. Look for more stories in the series—*Tell Me the Secrets, Tell Me the Truth, Tell Me the Promises,* and *Tell Me Why,* all published by Crossway Books—at your local bookstore.

COMING HOME

Text copyright © 1992, 2007 by Max Lucado
Illustrations copyright © 2007 by Justin Gerard
Published by Crossway Books
   a publishing ministry of
   Good News Publishers
   1300 Crescent Street
   Wheaton, Illinois 60187

Cover Design: Josh Dennis
Interior Design: Josh Dennis and The DesignWorks Group
Illustrations: Justin Gerard, Portland Studios

First printing 2007
Printed in the United States of America

LIBRARY OF CONGRESS CATALOGING-IN-PUBLICATION DATA

Lucado, Max.
 Coming home / Max Lucado ; illustrations by Justin Gerard.
  p. cm.
 "'Coming home' appeared originally as 'Before it's too late' in 'Tell me the story' written by Max Lucado and illustrated by Ron DiCianni"--T.p. verso.
 Summary: As shipwrecked brothers Argo and Arion wait on the silent, gray island of Terrene for their captain to return and take them to their new home, they ponder his warning about avoiding the local forest and mountain.
 ISBN-13: 978-1-58134-756-2 (hardcover : alk. paper)
 ISBN-10: 1-58134-756-1 (hardcover : alk. paper)
 [1. Brothers--Fiction. 2. Islands--Fiction. 3. Christian life--Fiction.] I. Gerard, Justin, ill. II. Title.
PZ7.L9684Com 2007
[E]--dc22
      2006018953

LB 15 14 13 12 11 10 09 08 07

15 14 13 12 11 10 9 8 7 6 5 4 3 2 1

FOR RUBEN AND SELMA

*Celebrating your love for kids
and devotion to God*

The two boys looked at the captain with astonishment.

"You're leaving the island?" they said in one voice, which they often did because they were twins and were always thinking the same thing.

"You can't leave the island!" Argo proclaimed. "Without you here we would be so . . . so . . ."

"Alone!" Arion completed Argo's sentence, as he often did.

"Arion is right!" Argo said.

The captain looked at the boys with kind eyes. "Just remember what I've taught you. And, remember, I'll be back."

The boys couldn't imagine life on Terrene without the captain. Argo and Arion were barely two years old the night their ship was wrecked. The captain and the boys drifted to this tiny island, made it their home, and named it Terrene. That was fourteen years ago. And now that the captain was leaving, they felt afraid.

"There's so much more to life than Terrene. And when I return, we'll leave together—for Bluestone."

More to life than Terrene? As far as Argo and Arion knew, everything in the world was just like Terrene—small and gray. Not a happy gray like the hue of shadowed snow. Not a strong gray like the shade of thunderclouds. But a dirty, dismal gray— like the worn skin of an elephant or the cold ashes of a dead fire.

"You've got to see with your heart—not your eyes," the captain would challenge.

The captain had spent many evenings sitting with the boys, explaining the grayness and the meaning of color. According to the captain, long ago a volcano had erupted, burying forever the colors of the isle under a blanket of soot.

As a result Terrene was a gray island in the middle of a big gray ocean. Waves with gray tips slapped against beaches with gray sand. Trees with gray trunks sheltered gray-winged birds. Gray animals with gray eyes peered from behind the gray bushes.

Only the boys and the captain were not gray.

A thick forest grew in the center of the island, and in the center of the forest there rose a mountain. The captain told the boys to stay away from both. "The volcano erupted once. It will erupt again. And stay out of the forest," he would say, "for the forest will take your color."

They believed the captain because he had seen a thousand islands. "There are islands," the captain told them, "so vast you cannot walk around them even in two days!"

This amazed Argo and Arion, for they could run all the way around Terrene in a few hours.

"And there are islands where the sky is so clear and the water so sweet that the birds sing, and the creatures leave the forest and come to the sand."

Amazing! Birds didn't sing on Terrene, and the creatures never left the forest.

"But there is one island that is most special."

"Bluestone!" the boys would state in unison. They knew the name well, for it was the captain's home.

"Ahh, Bluestone." The captain would smile. "There the birds always sing. Blue waters tumble over the shiny brown rocks, and the grass is ever green, and the sun sets on the horizon like an orange ball."

Argo and Arion would squeeze their eyes tight and try to picture the colors and hear the sounds. But they had never heard birds sing, and they'd only seen gray.

The captain knew it was hard; so he would help them. "Look at each other," he would venture. "See your blue eyes? That is the color of water at Bluestone. And see your blond hair? On my island there are birds and sunsets with such splendor. And your teeth—see how white? They are the color of Bluestone's sands. It's like nothing you've ever seen here in Terrene."

Then the captain would grow very solemn. "Argo, Arion, you were not made for Terrene. You were not made to live in the gray."

Then his voice would grow soft with sorrow. "Terrene was like Bluestone once—alive with sights and sounds—long ago, before the volcano."

But his voice would be sad only for a moment. "Bluestone is not gray." His eyes would dance as he spoke. "And Bluestone is your true home."

"I am going away for just a short time," he said. "I'm going to Bluestone to prepare your place. But I will come back and take you to be there with me."

"But what do we do while you are gone?" they asked.

"Remind each other that this is not your home. And help each other to be ready to leave when I return."

Though the boys believed the captain, their hearts were sad as he climbed in his fishing boat and set sail for Bluestone. "I will return!" he shouted to them. "Be ready!"

So began the days when Argo and Arion were alone together on the island.

At first they were just alike and did exactly the same things. They would rise early in the morning, look at each other's faces, and think of Bluestone.

"Your eyes are like the waters we will see," one would say.

"And your hair is yellow like the birds we will see," the other would answer.

"We were not made for Terrene," they reminded each other. "We were made for another place."

Then they would spend their day together, dreaming of the captain and remembering his words.

When evening came, they would go to the eastern beach from which the captain had sailed. There they would remember his farewell. "'I will come back and take you to be there with me,'" one would quote.

"'Be ready to leave when I return,'" the other would remind. And then they would rest for the night.

They spent many days searching the horizon for their captain. Looking for his return was their greatest joy . . . at first.

But after many days Argo and Arion began to grow tired.

"It's hard for me to remember his voice," Argo confessed.

Arion added, "The colors are getting blurry."

One afternoon Arion had gone to sleep on the gray sand while Argo took his turn at the watch. When Arion awoke, Argo had left the beach. He didn't return until the evening sun was setting, and Arion was already on the eastern coast.

"Where did you go?" Arion asked.

"I grew tired of the ocean and went into the forest."

"But the captain said to stay out of the forest. We need to stay together, Argo—to watch."

Argo didn't respond. And that evening when the two boys retold the words of the captain, Argo seemed uninterested.

When Arion awoke the next morning, Argo was gone again. Arion tried to see the colors and hear the music without the help of his brother, but it was hard. He felt alone, speaking into the sky with no one to listen, but he spoke anyway.

Several days passed before Arion saw his brother again. And when he did, Arion was shocked. He looked into Argo's eyes, longing to see the blue that would remind him of Bluestone, but the color was gone. Faded and pale was the hair that had been bright blond like the sun of the captain's country.

"Argo, you've changed!"

"No, I haven't," Argo argued.

"What's happened?"

"I've made some new friends in the forest. The animals. They aren't evil. They've shown me things I've never seen before. We swim in the river and run in the meadow and crawl in the cave beneath the great mountain."

"Argo, have you forgotten the captain's words? He said to stay away from the mountain. It could explode."

Argo laughed. "The creatures have told me the truth, Arion. The volcano never exploded, and it never will. That's just a fantasy. Come, I'll show you."

Arion looked at his brother for a long time. He looked at the eyes that used to sparkle and touched the hair that used to gleam. "You've changed, Argo. You are like the island."

"A little change doesn't hurt. Besides, what I'm doing in there is fun. Come with me."

"No, Argo, we must wait here. Maybe if you stay here, your color will return."

Argo laughed again. "Stay here and look for something that will never happen? And miss the fun of the forest? You're a fool, Arion. If the captain were returning, he'd be back by now. Come on and meet my friends."

"No, Argo. Stay with me and let me help you be ready for the captain's return."

The two brothers stood and looked at each other—Arion with sorrow and Argo with disbelief.

"You really think he's coming, don't you? After all this time? If you'd seen what I've seen in the forest, you wouldn't stay here on the beach."

"I've seen enough, Argo," Arion said sadly. "The forest has stolen your beauty. Stay with me. Change—before it's too late."

But Argo just smiled and walked toward the trees and became a part of the grayness.

A few days later a speck of gold appeared on the morning horizon—the color Argo's hair used to be, only a thousand times brighter. It sparkled and beamed like a fire in the night. The light cut through the gray with splendor. It was a grand schooner with billowed sails of purest white.

The captain had returned! Arion could see him on the bow of the ship.

"I'm back!" the captain called.

"I'm ready!" Arion shouted as loudly as he could. The captain waved.

When Arion boarded the ship, he raced into the captain's arms. The weariness of the watch was forgotten. What Arion had been able to see only with his heart, he now saw with his eyes.

He thought of his brother and looked up at the captain. "Argo chose Terrene."

Sadness came over the captain's face. He walked to the rail and looked at the gray forest.

Just as Arion was turning away, he saw movement. Argo! He saw his brother step hesitantly at first. And then he moved faster and faster until he reached the schooner.

"Argo," the captain said.

Argo glanced up at the tone of the captain's voice, but he quickly looked back down.

"You know now the deceptions of the forest," the captain said.

"Yes," Argo nodded. The captain looked at Argo for a long moment. Then Argo asked, "Please, may I come with you?"

The captain smiled and helped Argo
onto the ship.

The captain touched Argo on top of
the head, and Argo's hair shed its grayness,
and his eyes became blue as the waters at
Bluestone, and his body seemed to glow.

The ship set sail for Bluestone.
Only when they reached the horizon did they
feel the vibrations of the volcano erupting.

The Dread Isle of Terrene

Hidden Reef

The

Bottomless Channels

Palid Wastes

Volcano

Beach of Slate

Gray Forest

Terrene

Sinister Shoals

Sand Banks

Feral Foothills

Warren Cliffs